THOMAS & FRIENDS™

Chasing Rainbows

Based on a story by
Brandon Violette

Adapted by
Claire Sipi

First published in Great Britain 2023 by Farshore
An imprint of HarperCollins*Publishers*
1 London Bridge Street, London SE1 9GF
www.farshore.co.uk

HarperCollins*Publishers*
Macken House, 39/40 Mayor Street Upper, Dublin 1, D01 C9W8, Ireland

CREATED BY BRITT ALLCROFT

Based on the Railway Series by The Reverend W Awdry.
©2023 Gullane (Thomas) Limited. Thomas the Tank Engine & Friends™
and Thomas & Friends™ are trademarks of Gullane (Thomas) Limited.
©2023 HIT Entertainment Limited. HIT and the HIT logo are trademarks
of HIT Entertainment Limited.

ISBN 978 0 0085 3409 7
Printed in UK
001

A CIP catalogue record for this title is available from the British Library.

Stay safe online.
Farshore is not responsible for content hosted by third parties.

MIX
Paper | Supporting
responsible forestry
FSC™ C007454

This book is produced from independently certified FSC™ paper
to ensure responsible forest management.

For more information visit: www.harpercollins.co.uk/green

One cloudy day, Thomas and Kana were playing in the rain.

"The good thing about the rain," laughed Thomas, "is that however **muddy** I get, the rain washes me clean again!"

But just as Kana came **whizzing** by, **splashing** Thomas with mud, the rain suddenly stopped.
Uh oh!

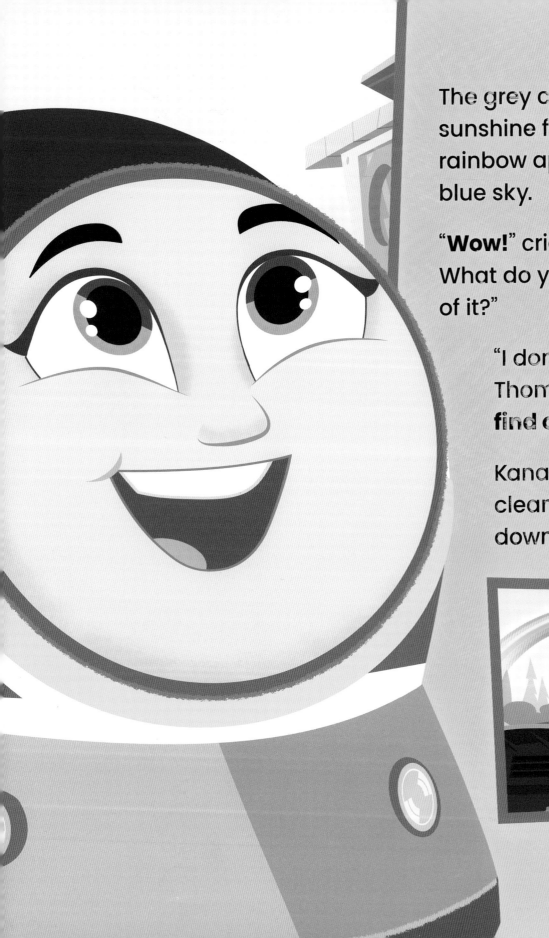

The grey clouds parted and sunshine filled the yard. A huge rainbow appeared in the bright blue sky.

"**Wow!**" cried Kana. "**A rainbow!** What do you think is at the end of it?"

"I don't know," peeped Thomas excitedly. "**Let's find out!**"

Kana helped Thomas get clean and they set off down the tracks.

The pair headed towards a little cottage where they could see the rainbow ended.

"I wonder what we'll find," said Thomas. "I hope it's shiny new wheels!"

"I hope it's golden headlights!" answered Kana, excitedly.

But when they arrived at the cottage, the rainbow had moved.

"That's odd," said Thomas. "Does the rainbow seem further away to you now?"

"Yes, it does," replied Kana. "**We can't let it get away!** Look, it's over by that tunnel."

The two engines **whizzed** off, but when they reached the tunnel, the rainbow had moved again.

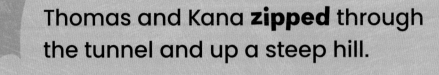

Thomas and Kana **zipped** through the tunnel and up a steep hill.

"Hello," puffed Percy, pulling up behind them. "What are you doing?"

"**We're chasing that rainbow**," cried Thomas. "But it keeps moving."

"**Cool**, I'll come with you. I've always wanted to see what's at the end of a rainbow," said Percy." I hope it's a new mailbag."

Thomas, Kana and Percy **raced** through the countryside.

"What are you doing?" called Nia, as she chugged past them.

"We're chasing a rainbow," peeped Thomas.

"Did this rainbow have **red**, **orange**, **yellow**, **green**, **blue**, **indigo** and **violet** colours? Because it's just over there," puffed Nia, pointing towards a tall mountain. "**Ooh**, I wonder what's at the end of it? Maybe a golden whistle!"

The engines **screeched** to a halt at the foot of the mountain. High above them, the end of the rainbow **glittered** brightly over the rocky peak.

"How are we going to get up there?" sighed Kana. **"The tracks are broken**. Now we'll never find out what's at the end of the rainbow."

Just then Diesel arrived. He had heard about the rainbow and had come along for the adventure. "We could ask Carly and Sandy to fix the track," said Diesel.

A short while later, Carly and Sandy arrived.

"With a **CLACK-CLACK** here," sang Carly.

"And a **SNAP-SNAP** there," replied Sandy.

"Here a-**CLACK**, there a-**SNAP**," they sang together.

In no time at all they had mended the broken tracks.

All the engines cheered.

"**Thanks Carly and Sandy!**" they cried.

"**FULL STEAM AHEAD!**" shouted Thomas. "Let's find out what's at the end of the rainbow!"

All the engines headed up the steep tracks ... It was a **LONG** way.

At last, they arrived at an old abandoned station sitting on top of the mountain. It glowed in the shimmering light of all the bright rainbow colours.

"The end of the rainbow!" whistled Thomas.

"Time to find out what our prizes are," giggled Kana.

The engines **zoomed** around the station excitedly, each looking for their rainbow prizes.

"I don't see a golden whistle," said Nia.

"I can't find any gold headlights," said Kana.

"I guess there's nothing at the end of the rainbow after all ..." sighed a disappointed Nia.

"I think I've found something!" shouted Thomas from a platform above the old station. "**Up here!**"

All the engines raced up to the platform to see what Thomas had found.

"I wonder what it is?" said Diesel.

"I really hope it's a pot of sand!" said Sandy.

"Or a new hook!" giggled Carly.

Everyone gathered around Thomas. They peered out over the mountain edge to see **the most amazing sight**. Below them they could see the whole of the island of Sodor.

Thomas grinned at his friends. "This would make a great secret clubhouse for the Biggest Adventure Club!"

"This is way better than golden headlights or shiny wheels," sighed Kana, "because it's something **we can all share**."

"Every secret clubhouse needs a name," smiled Percy. "What shall we call ours?"

"Let's call it 'Lookout Mountain'," replied Thomas, "since we can see everything from up here."

Everyone cheered.

"See, there really was treasure at the end of the rainbow!"